CINDERELLA
And Other Stories

Retold by *Jeanne Cappe*

Illustrated by *J. L. Huens*

Translated from the French
by *Marie Ponsot*

GROSSET & DUNLAP · NEW YORK

Stories in this Book
Cinderella
Puss In Boots
Donkey Skin
The Fairies

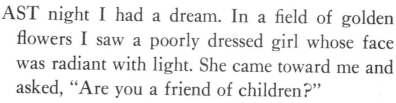

AST night I had a dream. In a field of golden flowers I saw a poorly dressed girl whose face was radiant with light. She came toward me and asked, "Are you a friend of children?"

"I certainly am," I answered. I showed her the snapshots in my wallet — the ones of Jacqueline, of John on his bike, of Tom near the campfire at Scout Camp, eating a roasted potato.

"Yes, I believe you," the girl said. "But don't you recognize me?"

I'd noticed her slippers among the flowered grass, and had just been asking myself, "Where have I seen them before?"

"Of course!" I suddenly knew. "You're Cinderella!"

"Yes, I am," she said. "And do you know why I have not worn my finery, save for my slippers, and put these rags back on? I might have come to you in the marvelous gowns I wore to the Prince's ball, but . . ."

"But," I interrupted, "you like to dress in the old tatters once in a while, to remind you that there is a sweetness in being poor, and that your wicked, lazy sisters, despite their jewels and comforts, were far less rich in joy than you."

"You're right!" exclaimed Cinderella. "Nothing could have taken away the pleasure I had in doing whatever I had to do just as well as I could. Richness is not just a question of having a kingdom, and servants, and many clothes . . . but I didn't come to talk about myself. I wanted to ask you — is it true that children don't like fairy stories any more?"

"Whoever tried to tell you such a silly thing?" I asked. I was very cross. "Maybe it was Puss in Boots — he's said so many untrue things!"

"Someone talking about me?" said a voice from an apple tree. Puss in Boots came down with a bound — boots, sack, and all. He doffed his plumed hat, held it over his heart, and gallantly declared, "I protest, if you please; for if I told the King that the game I caught had been taken by my master, and that the fields all belonged to the Marquis of Carabas, it was only to give you one more good story to tell the children. You need an imagination like mine to make children glad!"

"A magic wand does as well," said another voice. There came Donkey Skin, wearing her wonderful weather-colored dress.

"You know," she said, "the Fairies always do things just right, which is why children love them. But they do nothing without our cooperation. Even though I had a Fairy Godmother, I fed pigs, cleaned stables, and worked hard, before I met the Prince of my dreams."

She drew from beneath her splendid sleeve a fine, strong hand, saying, "There, you see, that's the real magic wand."

Just then the golden flowers about us grew and grew and grew, and each flower became a Fairy.

"The children love us still, don't they," said the Fairies, "when they hear fairy tales?"

"Of course," I said. "And when I told them that one of the Fairies gave a kindly girl the gift of speaking with a shower of pearls and flowers, they decided to have only generous thoughts in their hearts."

And then, young friends, I awoke. Cinderella, Puss in
Boots, Donkey Skin and the Fairies, had disappeared.
"I must bring them back," I thought. So I took
my pen and began to write, once again, the
enchanting tales of good Mr. Perrault.

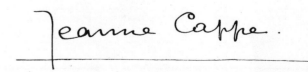

Cinderella

ONCE there was a girl just as brave as she was beautiful. She was very sad, sometimes, when she thought of her mother, who had died, and her father, whom a wicked woman had married, and of the tender, happy life she used to have. But she knew that patience always wins at last; and her godmother, who was a Fairy, assured her that difficult days are often the price of bright tomorrows.

Every morning, Cinderella was the first one up. She cleaned the whole house, and cleared up the frightful disorder left by her stepsisters — for her father's second wife had two daughters as haughty as their mother.

Having worked through the long day, Cinderella would sit at the hearth and turn over the cinders to keep the fire ablaze. For that reason the wicked sisters called her Cindersitter, which became Cinderella.

One day the King's son announced that he was going to give a ball. Cinderella's two sisters, who went to every possible party, were invited. For days and days they fussed, deciding what would be most beautiful to wear. They were forever in front of a mirror, though it made them not a bit prettier. Their mother, who was going with them, spent all her time in the same way, buying things and trying them on. You can see from this ridiculous behavior how silly they were, all three.

They told Cinderella to arrange their hair. She did it, as she did everything, better than anyone else. In their nasty way her stepsisters schemed to make her jealous.

"Don't you wish you could go to the ball, Cinderella?" they teased.

"You know I couldn't do that" poor Cinderella answered.

The wicked sisters roared with laughter. "Of course you can't — a Cinder-sitter at the Prince's ball! That would be too, too ridiculous!"

And they snickered and sneered.

Cinderella might have taken revenge by pulling their hair, just a little, while she fixed it. But she was so good that she thought only of doing her best for them.

At last, it was the night of the ball, and the sisters burst from the house in a tizzy.

Left alone, Cinderella wept. She never, never had a chance for fun — never a party, never a ball, not even a picnic.

Her Fairy Godmother took pity and came to keep her company at the hearth. "Tell me, Cinderella, would you like to go to the Prince's ball?" she asked.

"Oh, yes, Godmother!" said Cinderella between two sobs.

"Well, then," the Fairy said, "go into the garden and find me a pumpkin."

Cinderella obeyed, hardly daring to wonder just how a pumpkin might help her get to the ball.

The Fairy hollowed out the big round fruit, and struck it with her wand. The pumpkin turned at once into a magnificent golden carriage.

Next, she went to fetch a mousetrap, and opened it. One by one the mice came out. As each one appeared, a tap from the Fairy's magic wand transformed it into a beautiful dapple-gray horse.

Now nothing was missing but a coachman and servants. Cinderella suggested that her godmother look in the rattrap to see if anything were caught there. She found that it held three fat rats, which the wand changed, quick as a flash, into a coachman and two footmen. Then the Fairy turned six little lizards into pageboys.

"There!" said the godmother to her godchild. "Now you can get to the ball! Are you satisfied?"

"Oh, yes, of course," said Cinderella; but she looked down at her tattered clothes in hope that the good Fairy might understand that such rags were not fit for a palace.

Surprise! The magic wand had scarcely touched her when she found herself robed in an exquisite dress, a necklace of the finest pearls, and a pair of adorable little slippers lined with ermine.

"Now run along," said her godmother. "Have a glorious time at your first ball. But remember, you must leave before the stroke of midnight. If you stay any later, your

carriage will turn back into a pump-kin, your horses will become mice, your coachman and footmen will be rats, and your pageboys, lizards; and you, my dear, will be dressed once more in rags."

The ball was in full swing when someone came to tell the Prince that a magnificently dressed Princess of striking beauty had just stepped down from her carriage. He hurried to meet the newcomer, and led her by the hand among his guests. Their entrance made such a sensation that the musicians stopped playing, and the dancers stood still.

"How lovely she looks! How sweet she seems!" the elderly ladies murmured behind their fans.

The King himself said over and over to the Queen that, in all his many years, he had never yet seen so beautiful a girl.

The young ladies, who are often like monkeys, because monkey-like, many of them imitate everything they see, inspected the pretty guest carefully so that they might copy her dress and hairdo the very next day.

The King's son was enchanted, and started the ball again by dancing with the new arrival. She danced with such grace that everyone who saw her was completely charmed.

The wicked sisters were seated under a balcony, where hardly anyone came to speak with them because they looked so disagreeable. Cinderella joined them, and offered them some sugared almonds the Prince had given her. They were somewhat astonished at the kindness shown to them by this Princess, whom they never suspected was the very same Cinder-sitter who did all their household chores.

When it was a quarter to twelve, Cinderella took care to be on her way. Without her, the party lost most of its joy.

Back at home, she saw her godmother once more, and asked if she might go to the ball again the next night. The King's son had beseeched her to do so, and she did not wish to offend him.

Just then a knock was heard at the door, and the Fairy vanished. It was the wicked sisters and their mother coming back. Cinderella pretended to be just waking up, and yawned and yawned.

"If you had been at the ball with us," said one of the sisters, "you would have seen the most beautiful Princess in the world. Her dress was simply splendid, and the plain way she wore her hair just made her seem more elegant."

"Did she seem nice?" asked Cinderella.

"Certainly she did. She gave us almonds, and said all kinds of nice things to us."

"What was her name?" Cinderella asked her stepsisters.

"Nobody knows," they answered. "After she left, the Prince said he'd give half his kingdom to know who she is."

"How I should like to have seen her!" said Cinderella. "Won't one of you lend me just an everyday dress, so that I may come with you to the ball tomorrow night?"

"Silly girl!" they hooted nastily. "As if we'd lend anything to an ugly Cinder-sitter like you!"

Cinderella had expected no better. In fact, she would have been far from pleased had one of her stepsisters agreed to lend her a gown.

The King's son spent the next day in a state of impatience hoping to see the fair Princess again. Until he could do that, he would look at no one. When she did appear, she was even more beautifully dressed than before. The Prince led her into the garden where he could enjoy talking with her. For Cinderella had suffered, and done a deal of thinking, and so could talk of better matters than gossip and nonsense.

The Prince, too, had many interesting and intelligent ideas. Cinderella liked hearing him talk. She liked it so well, in fact, that she forgot the time.

As the first stroke of midnight sounded, she rose and fled; and in her haste she lost one of her little ermine-lined slippers. The Prince, who had followed to ask her to stay, stopped to pick up the delicate shoe. Alas! She had disappeared. He asked the guards, but they had seen only a poor girl in tatters who was nothing like a Princess. Holding the slipper fast, the Prince — who was now more intrigued than ever — planned how to find the unknown Princess again.

The next day the wicked sisters again told Cinderella about the wonderful ball, and the midnight flight of the beautiful maiden.

"She lost her slipper," they added, "and the Prince did nothing but stare at that tiny shoe. He certainly seemed in love with its owner."

Some days later an announcement went out to the whole kingdom. The Prince had declared that he would marry the girl whose foot would fit perfectly into the little ermine-lined slipper. One of his officers had the duty of going from house to house to try the slipper on every maiden in the kingdom.

Princesses, Duchesses, Countesses, gentlemen's daughters, all tried to put on the slipper — but in vain. Truth to tell, to fit that slipper would take a very small foot indeed.

Eventually the Palace Officer came to knock at the door of Cinderella's sisters, who hurried to try it on; but they had bigger feet than most girls their age.

Cinderella recognized her slipper, and came close. The wicked sisters couldn't wait to see which one could make the most fun of her.

"Do you suppose, you

Cinder-sitter, that you are good enough to be worthy of marrying the King's son?'' they sneered.

"I beg your pardon," said the officer, "but my orders are to try the slipper on every maiden in the kingdom." And he knelt before Cinderella.

The slipper fitted her to perfection.

At that very moment her Fairy Godmother appeared. One touch of her magic wand and Cinderella stood splendid before them, gowned as she had been for the ball.

The wicked sisters could only humbly beg her pardon for all their meanness to her. But the gentle Cinderella said that she recalled nothing of the kind and assured them that they would always be dear to her.

She who was Cinder-sitter no longer, since she was engaged to the King's son, went to stay at the palace. The wedding took place soon after. There, Cinderella introduced her sisters to two charming gentlemen who made them better by making them happy.

As for the little ermine-lined slippers, they were put on exhibit in a glass case. They were a constant reminder to the Prince and Princess that their happiness had begun one night, without their knowing it, at the first stroke of midnight.

Puss In Boots

THERE was once a young man in a very sad state of mind. His father had recently died, leaving him only a cat. One of his brothers had inherited the father's mill, and the other, a donkey.

"If my brothers work together, they'll earn an honest living," thought the young man. "But how will I make use of this cat?"

"Easier than you think, Master," said the cat, who had been only half asleep. "Give me my way and I promise to make you a fortune. I'll need a sack and a pair of boots, and then you'll see."

The young man knew that his cat was a very clever fellow, and decided to trust him. Puss got his boots, and a sack as well.

Thus equipped, Puss went out to hide in a briar patch that was simply alive with rabbits. There was a little grain in the bottom of his sack, and he had a shrewd plan in mind. He lay, eyes half shut, pretending to be dead, until he saw a foolish rabbit slip into his sack to eat the grain. He shut the sack quickly and put an end to the unlucky rabbit. An hour later he presented himself before the King.

"Sire,"
said Puss
with his most ex-
quisite bow, "in ac-
cordance with the orders
of my master, the Marquis of
Carabas, I offer you this fine rabbit
from his game reserve."

There was, of course, no Marquis of Carabas. Puss had invented the title just to impress
people with his master's seeming nobility.

The King was naturally flattered by the gift. He sent
its donor thousands of kind remarks, along with his most
generous thanks.

The next day Puss took his sack and went hunting again. This time
he caught two pheasant. He took them at once to the King as a present
from the Marquis of Carabas. The King thanked him again, and ordered
that Puss be given a magnificent feast.

So from time to time Puss brought to the court game that, said Puss,
his master had hunted. The King and his courtiers came to know quite
well the name of the Marquis of Carabas. Puss most certainly knew what
he was doing!

One day he heard that the King expected to go for a drive along
the river. He suggested to his master that he bathe at a certain spot, and
follow all Puss' instructions exactly.

Scarcely was the so-called Marquis well wet when the royal party
came along. The cat immediately began to call, "Help, help! The Marquis of Carabas is drowning!"

Hearing the hubbub, the King stuck his royal head from out the
carriage window. He recognized Puss, who had brought him so many
presents, and gave orders to rush to the aid of the poor Marquis. While
he was being helped from the river, Puss told the monarch that thieves

had stolen his master's clothes while he bathed. The Palace Officer of the Wardrobe was promptly sent off and ordered to return with a set of rich clothes befitting the Marquis of Carabas — which he did at once.

He looked so splendid when he had put them on that His Majesty treated him with especial courtesy. As for the King's daughter, the Princess fell in love right off, and gazed at him with great rapture.

The King then insisted that the Marquis join him in his private carriage and share the pleasures of the drive.

Puss went on ahead of them. He met some farmers cutting grain in the fields and said to them, "If you do not tell whoever asks that these fields belong to the Marquis of Carabas, I will have you ground into mincemeat!"

The farmers naturally dreaded such a fate; thus, when the King asked in whose fields they were working, they replied, like a trained choir, "Sire, these fields belong to the Marquis of Carabas."

"A superb piece of property," nodded the King to the supposed Marquis.

Puss, still well ahead of the King and his party, saw some harvesters.

"Ho, there!" he called. "If you do not proclaim that these fields belong to the Marquis of Carabas, I will have you ground into mincemeat!"

The frightened harvesters told the King, when he asked, that the length and breadth of their harvests belonged person- ally to the Marquis of Carabas.

Puss threatened every farmer for many miles around, and ordered them to give the same answers, so that the King was astonished at the richness of the Marquis' holdings.

At length, Puss came to a castle where lived the richest of all ogres. He entered it and told the ogre that he did not wish to pass by without paying his respects.

"For," Puss went on, "I've heard that you can change yourself into all kinds of animals."

"Quite so," said the ogre proudly. "For instance, I can be a lion."

And with just a couple of magic words the ogre did indeed change into an enormous lion. The cat was terrified. He wanted to scurry up the drainpipe, but he soon thought of a better way out of the problem.

"Ah, yes," said Puss. "You are big and strong; it's fairly easy for you to become some powerful beast. But if you could change yourself into some tiny creature — a mouse, now, or a rat, for instance — that would be really extraordinary."

"Not extraordinary at all," the vain ogre answered.

He said some mysterious words, and became a mouse. Puss was ready and waiting. He leaped on the mouse and devoured him.

Then he licked his lips and went to the drawbridge to await the coming of the royal carriage. When he saw it, he cried, "Welcome to the castle of the Marquis of Carabas, Your Majesty!"

The amazed King asked to be shown everything. In one huge room a sumptuous meal had been prepared, quite as if the King had been expected. In truth, it was the ogre who had planned the feast for a dinner with friends that day.

Around the table, the King, the Princess, and our supposed Marquis had a gay meal. They ate and drank with such delight that after half an hour the King said confidentially, "I should be not at all displeased to have a son-in-law like you, Marquis."

His daughter, hearing these words, appeared to agree, and her eyes brightened to show how pleased she was.

The cat smiled into his whiskers.

So the Marquis of Carabas married the daughter of the King. They were very happy, and had lots of children, all of whom learned to respect the cat as a lord and to love him as a friend.

Donkey Skin

*O*NCE there was a King who had everything a man needed for contentment. His kingdom was large, prosperous, and at peace; his subjects were loyal and devoted. His household was happy, year in and year out, thanks to his wife, the Queen, who was blessed with every good quality. Their happiness was made perfect by the birth of a lovely little Princess.

Let me add that in the rich, luxurious palace of this King there was one remarkable thing. It was a donkey: a donkey who was kept, not in the stable, but in a most elegant suite of rooms. And why, do you think, was this? It was because this donkey had a very rich Fairy Godmother who left pieces of gold under the donkey's pillow every night. The King, therefore, was extremely rich, and since he was also very generous with his wealth, he was thought a very good King.

But a great shadow darkened all this joy. The Queen fell so ill that there was no hope for her life. Dying, she said to the King, "Promise me, if you marry again, to choose no wife who has not all of the good qualities that you have found in me."

The King told her tearfully that he would be too grief-stricken to even dream of replacing her.

When she had died, he did weep, so hard and loud that at first it seemed he would never recover. He was completely saddened by the loss of his Queen and it was several years before he was able to return to his kingly duties and the affairs of state.

And so, the time passed. Years later, however, when the King had become an old man, he thought of remarrying.

His promise to
the Queen made his
choice difficult. He
looked in every kingdom,
every city, every farmland, every
palace, every mansion. He had to ad-
mit that no one matched his late Queen's
qualities.

One day, while he was being taken for a drive
through his estates, he saw an enchanting young lady pick-
ing flowers in the countryside. She was a kind and beautiful
Princess, and the daughter of a neighboring King. So much did she
resemble his late Queen, that the King declared he would marry her.

It's easy to imagine how sad the Princess was at the news. She was
very young, and more befitting for a dashing Prince than the King, who
now was old and wrinkled. In despair she went to that most admirable
Fairy, her godmother.

The Fairy knew what was the matter, and told her not to worry.

"Don't let the old King know you are against his wishes. Instead,
you and I will find ways to keep him out of such foolishness. Suppose
you ask him for something impossible to get — for instance, a dress the
color of weather. He has power and wealth, but where could he find a
weather-colored dress?"

So the Princess asked the King for a dress the color of weather.
The King at once summoned the best tailors in his kingdom to carry
out this wish. Two days had not dawned when they delivered the dress.
How splendid it was! It seemed to be spun of the sky's blue, the sun's
gold, the cloud's rose, butterfly's wings, and the rarest flower colors. The
Princess was speechless with admiration — and with fear. She had never
imagined that the King could fulfill her request.

Her godmother saw her perplexity and whispered softly, "Now
ask for a dress the color of the moon!"

The King conveyed this wish to the embroiderers and ordered the dress to be ready in four days.

And it was. The Princess was breathless to see a gown that blended the silvery shadows and silver stars of the fairest night imaginable.

Admiring, but embarrassed, the Princess wouldn't have known what to do if the Fairy hadn't prompted her to ask for a third dress — this time, the color of the sun.

The King summoned a jeweler and told him to accomplish the Princess' wish before the week was out. The designer was so clever and the workers so diligent that the work was done ahead of time. It was a perfect wonder, a masterpiece that dazzled all eyes.

The Princess didn't know what to do next to get out of her difficult situation.

"You can see," she said to her godmother, "that the King manages to grant even the most extraordinary wishes."

"No doubt," she replied. "As long as the donkey, through its godmother, gives the King unlimited gold to pay artists and workers, he'll be able to make good his promises. So now you must ask him to give you the donkey's skin."

The King hesitated not a second to sacrifice the means of his

wealth for the Princess' pleasure.

Then how downcast she was! She took her troubles to the Fairy, who said, "Those who are on the path of goodness and truth have nothing to fear. There is but one thing left to do: disguise yourself and run away. Here is a big trunk. Put all your things into it, along with your three lovely dresses and your diamonds and rubies. And here is my magic wand. The minute you tap the ground with it, the trunk will appear, for it will follow you underground wherever you go. Finally, so that you may not be recognized, put mud on your face and cover yourself with the donkey skin. Who could ever guess, in that disguise, that you are really so fine and fair a Princess!"

So it was done. The Princess fled far and far, hidden under the donkey skin. They sought her in vain, but no one could find her.

At last she came to a farm where the farmer's wife needed someone to scrub the dishcloths and the pig's trough. When she saw the Princess all soiled and stained, she thought her well fit for such work and hired her at once.

The poor girl, pushed into a kitchen corner, began a hard life. While some mocked her, others wouldn't even speak to her. They thought her repulsively ugly and, cloaked as she was, called her Donkey Skin.

On Sundays, Donkey Skin would have a little rest. She would go to her little hut, carefully close the door, clean the mud from her face, and open her trunk. Her one joy was to dress up, perhaps in her weather-colored dress, or in her moon-colored dress, or in her dress the color of the sun. She would gaze into her mirror and bravely think more of the good the future might hold than of the sorrow of the past.

From one Sunday to the next the weeks sped by. Donkey Skin hoped her woes would soon end, and it was this hope that made her work seem lighter.

The farm where the poor Princess lived in disguise, was part of a castle in which a King sometimes came to live. In an immense cage, and around the barnyard, he kept a collection of rare birds and fowl. There were quail and cormorants, Barbary chickens and tropical humming-birds, enough to fill dozens of birdhouses.

This King had a son who was fond of taking a stroll among the curious creatures of this fabulous collection. Donkey Skin would see him there, and she soon noticed how attractive he was, and how his face shone with kindness when he fed the birds.

"If he's engaged," she sighed, "how happy the girl must be! To be in her place, I'd exchange all my splendid clothes for the simplest old dress."

One Sunday, as the Prince wandered through the barnyards, he passed the door of a little room. Curious, he looked through the key-hole. He stood amazed, for there he saw a girl gowned in a most marvelous dress, covered with fabulous jewels, and unbelievably beautiful as well. He watched her for a long

time. Her sad, brave expression went straight to his heart. Three times he wanted to open the door, and three times drew back. Was it merely a vision, or was it a dream?

He found the farmer's wife and asked who was the exquisite young girl in the miserable hut off in the corner of the barnyard.

"Exquisite young girl!" she sputtered. "But that's Donkey Skin, our unsightly maid-of-all-work!"

The Prince was left with this puzzle. He had seen the splendid girl with his own eyes. He thought only of her, so hard and so much that he fell ill. His worried mother begged him to tell her his troubles. He would only say that he wanted Donkey Skin to make him a cake with her own hands.

His mother had never heard of Donkey Skin. She inquired at the farm, where they said she must mean their maid-of-all-work, who was as homely as a newborn duckling.

"What does it matter?" said the Queen. "My son is ill. We must satisfy his every whim." She loved him so much that if he had asked for gold to eat, she'd have given him some.

Donkey Skin was told to make a cake for the Prince. She took flour, butter, and fresh eggs, and went to her hut to mix the batter.

She stirred and mixed so busily that she did not notice her ring slip off her finger and drop into the bowl. It was an incredibly fine ring of gold, shaped like a reed, and mounted with a flawless emerald.

Eating the cake, the Prince was so lost in dreams that he might have swallowed the ring. But he felt something hard, discovered it, and believed it to be a sign of good omen. He hid it under his pillow.

The Queen saw him grow weaker and weaker, and lamented long and loud. The doctors said, as they often do when they don't know what else to suggest, "He should get married!"

The Prince was cross at first, but then he said, "I'm willing to marry, on one condition: my bride must be the one whom this ring fits."

The King and Queen thought this very odd, but since their son was so sick they dared not say no.

Heralds went throughout the kingdom to announce that any woman might come to try her finger in the ring. In that way, the Prince's bride would be selected.

Soon everyone knew that the ring was so tiny it would fit only the slenderest of fingers. Doctors and sorcerers were begged for potions and magical powers to make the fingers thin.

The trial of the ring was conducted with great ceremony. First Princesses, then Marquises, then Duchesses, were admitted. Their fingers were small, but not small enough for the ring.

Next to try it on came Baronnesses and Countesses, and other noble gentlewomen, then the daughters of commoners, then servants, cooks, and goose-girls. Each time, in each case, the finger was too fat for the ring. Not one could get it on.

"And Donkey Skin?" said the Prince.

Everyone burst out laughing. Still giggling, someone fetched the maid-of-all-work from her barnyard corner. The laughter suddenly stopped when they saw the maiden extend, from under the donkey skin, a small, small hand that looked as if it were made of rose-ivory.

The ring was tried — and on it slipped, right at home, on the slenderest finger ever seen. They wanted to present her to the King at once, but she said she would wait until she had dressed properly.

They all thought she would dress, at best, as a goose-girl. How they all gasped to see her enter the royal dwelling — a girl gowned in a magnificent dress the color of the sun!

The good King was enchanted with her beauty, her splendor, and her grace. The Queen was utterly astonished. As for the Prince, he grew well at once, and thanked Heaven for the joy in his heart.

Elaborate preparations were made for the wedding. The ruler invited the Crown Heads of every state,

yes, every single King from every land, far and wide. There were Kings who wore speckled ostrich plumes, or tasseled velvet turbans, or golden leopard capes. There came too, without knowing who the bride was to be, the old King who had wished to marry this same Princess.

When he saw the bride, he was stupefied to recognize his once beloved. Of course, he was delighted to see her again. He himself had come to his senses after the Princess had disappeared, and remarried a widowed Queen full of good qualities who was closer to his own age.

At this point, the Fairy Godmother appeared. She told of Donkey Skin's trials and bravery, and the tale added to the glory of the young bride. The wedding was the wonderful start of many long years of happiness. And since every King from every kingdom in the world attended the ceremony, it is believed that throughout the entire universe the story of Donkey Skin is known and told, in every language, to every single child.

The Fairies

A WOMAN once had two daughters.

The elder one resembled her. Fanchon was her name. She had, like her mother, a mean heart, and a disagreeable face that reflected her horrid nature.

The other daughter, Mary, was sweet, honest, and kind. She was like her father, who had died.

The mother preferred Fanchon, who was very lazy. Fanchon could sleep as late as she wished in the morning. But Mary, the younger girl, had to rise early to do the housework, the washing, and all the heavy jobs. Mary also had to go to a well quite far from the house to fetch water twice a day. It was tiring work, but the girl always went at it happily and would sing with a willing heart.

One day, as Mary was filling her pitchers, a poor old woman came up and asked her for a drink.

"With pleasure," she smiled good-naturedly, and dipped the pitcher into the clearest part of the well. When Mary brought up the fresh water, she tipped the pitcher forward so that the old woman might drink with ease.

"How kind and helpful you are, and smiling too," said the old woman. "I should like to give you a nice present, in return."

But Mary said she had done no more than her duty, and wished she might do something more to help.

She didn't know that she had just given a drink to an exceedingly

powerful Fairy, who had dressed as a poor peasant woman to see if there were any good people left on earth. "From now on," said the Fairy, "at each word you speak a flower or a precious jewel will fall from your lips."

When Mary got home, her mother scolded her because she had taken so long to get water. Mary began to apologize, saying that she had met a poor old woman, when — lo and behold — jewels fell from her lips, and then roses, and then pearls!

Her greedy mother, overjoyed at sight of the rich gems, asked what had happened. Mary shyly told of the old woman's gift.

When her mother learned what had taken place, she was overcome with more greed and ordered her elder daughter off to the well.

At first Fanchon refused to go, and left grouchily only after her mother insisted. Too lazy to carry anything heavy, she took no pitcher, but just a silver vase.

She had scarcely reached the well when a richly dressed lady came and asked if she would be so gracious as to give her a drink. Once more, it was the Fairy, dressed in disguise.

"Oh, you!" said Fanchon as rudely as she could. "Do you think

I'm here just to give you a drink? Get one of your maids to help you."

"My dear girl! How unpleasant you are," said the lady. "I'm going to give you a suitable gift. Every time you open your mouth, toads, snakes, and scorpions will tumble out."

Fanchon shrugged her shoulders and went home. When her mother saw her, she called, "Well, daughter?"

"Well, what?" she said crudely. As she spoke, two toads and a snake tumbled forth from her mouth.

"A terrible curse!" cried her mother. "It's Mary's fault, I'm sure. My poor, dear Fanchon!" And she spanked and spanked Mary until the poor girl finally fled into the depths of the forest, determined never to go home again.

Mary wandered for a long time without hope of finding food or shelter. But as night came on she saw a light gleaming through the trees. It led her to a cabin. Entering, she saw a bed, and a table set with food. Mary expected that the owners would return any minute. But it grew pitch-dark, and still no one came. Finally, she ate a little and went to bed.

While she slept, Fairies spoke to her in dreams. They said the cabin was for her, and that she might live there to await her destiny.

Mary had noticed that everything was brand-new, and when she awoke in the morning, knowing that all of it belonged to her, her heart overflowed with thanks. She joyously put everything in her new home in place, and later, finding some material, needles, and thread, did a little sewing.

When she had worked long enough, she went for a walk through the woods. On a side path she found a deer,

hurt by hunters, and moaning with teary eyes. She tore her handkerchief into strips and bandaged the poor creature's wound. Then she came on a fallen fledgling bird and put it back in its nest. She next noticed a brook almost stopped up with papers and twigs, and hurried to clear them away so that the water could flow along, fresh and free. So Mary, even when alone, found a thousand kindly things to do.

Yet, it was hard to live by herself in the depths of the forest, with never the sight of another human being. She would have liked someone to talk to, someone to love and cherish.

The days passed. Mary felt so lonely that one afternoon she went and sat beneath a tree and cried, until at last she fell asleep on the moss, still shaken by sobs.

The King's son, out hunting, chanced to pass that way. He was moved to see the beautiful girl whose face, even in sleep, was wet with tears. As he was gazing sympathetically at her, she awoke. He asked why she was sad.

"Sir," she said, "my mother treated me cruelly, so I left her house. I've lived for some time in a cabin in a little clearing. My only friends are the forest creatures."

As she spoke, the Fairy's gift of diamonds and pearls fell in a shower about her. The King's son marveled as Mary told him her whole story, gently and simply as ever.

The Prince very soon found himself completely in love with Mary. Her goodness seemed to him a treasure even greater than the jewels that sprang from her lips. He asked to marry her, and when Mary said she would, brought her to the palace. A few days later the wedding — a truly splendid wedding — took place.

When Fanchon heard how happy Providence had made Mary, she turned sick with envy. She grew as yellow as a lemon, and she and her mother lived very unhappily, never content either with themselves or with anyone else. And the toads, snakes, and scorpions never ceased to tumble from that mouth of hers, which had never spoken a kind word to anyone.